Pirate Queen
A Story of Zheng Yi Sao

Helaine Becker

PICTURES BY
Liz Wong

GROUNDWOOD BOOKS
HOUSE OF ANANSI PRESS
TORONTO BERKELEY

The publisher would like to thank Dian Murray, PhD, for checking the text
and illustrations.

Groundwood Books / House of Anansi Press
groundwoodbooks.com

We gratefully acknowledge for their financial support of our publishing
program the Canada Council for the Arts, the Ontario Arts Council and the
Government of Canada.

Canada Council   Conseil des Arts
for the Arts   du Canada

ONTARIO ARTS COUNCIL
CONSEIL DES ARTS DE L'ONTARIO
an Ontario government agency
un organisme du gouvernement de l'Ontario

With the participation of the Government of Canada | Canadä
Avec la participation du gouvernement du Canada

Library and Archives Canada Cataloguing in Publication

Title: Pirate queen : a story of Zheng Yi Sao / Helaine Becker ;
pictures by Liz Wong.
Other titles: Story of Zheng Yi Sao
Names: Becker, Helaine, author. | Wong, Liz, illustrator.
Identifiers: Canadiana (print) 20190148012 | Canadiana (ebook)
20190148187 | ISBN 9781773061245 (hardcover) |
ISBN 9781773061252 (EPUB) | ISBN 9781773063560 (Kindle)
Subjects: LCSH: Zhèng, Shì, 1775-1844—Juvenile literature. |
LCSH: Pirates—Biography—Juvenile literature.
Classification: LCC G537.Z54 P57 2020 | DDC j364.16/4092—dc23

The illustrations were done in pencil on bristol board and colored digitally.
Design by Michael Solomon
Printed and bound in Malaysia

MIX
Paper from
responsible sources
FSC® C012700

For Sheila Barry, who is greatly missed — HB

For my sister, Jen — LW

$\mathcal{I}$ never dreamed of the sea.

I never, not in my wildest imaginings, fancied myself a pirate queen.

But Fortune cares nothing for your dreams. She takes up your life in her cup and shakes it so hard your teeth rattle in your head and your heart roars like a dragon in your chest. Then she throws the bones onto her table of lacquer and jade.

Your fate is sealed.

So there I sat, combing my hair, unaware that the pirates had landed.

Or that they tore through the city, smashing windows, kicking dogs, looting and fighting and killing. Searching for someone like me.

Their captain, Zheng Yi, had set before them this task: to bring him a girl to wed.

The pirates stormed our homes.
We girls scattered like chickens in the
rain. We squawked like chickens, too.
But there was no chance to escape.

They carried us like sacks of rice
across their backs. No one answered
our cries for help.

At the quay, they lowered us into
rowboats, along with other stolen
goods.

We were not treated with tenderness.
That was reserved for the casks of new
wine.

In the distance, the rigging of the
pirate ship sketched strange characters
across the face of the Jade Rabbit.

The oars splished.

The other girls wailed and vomited.

I felt neither fear nor seasickness.
Nor any sorrow.

In Canton, girls like us were like ink:
used and used until we were all used
up.

But Fortune had shaken my bones and spun the wheel of my fate.

I had been given something rare: an opportunity.

I was ink, but I could also be the brush.

If Fortune allowed, I would write my own scroll.

I refused to marry Captain Zheng Yi unless he gave me an equal share in his enterprise.

The pirate king laughed at my boldness. But he agreed. Perhaps because he'd seen his fate scrawled across the face of the Jade Rabbit.

Within six years, my new husband was dead.

His lieutenant Zhang Bao was loyal but better at
taking orders than conceiving them. I didn't give him
the chance. Before my husband's body slipped under
the waves, I took command of the fleet.

I issued orders.

Established rules.

Distributed favors.

No one challenged me.

Not even Zhang Bao.

I was now thirty-two years old. A widow. And the queen of 70,000 men, with more than 1,800 ships at my command.

Fortune had lifted me high and flung me headlong into the teeth of the wind.

I stood tall astride the bow, the salt spray mingling with my tears.

They were tears of pride. And also, I admit, of terror.

I thought I saw my husband's face smiling up at me from the inky depths, encouraging me.

How long before the waves washed my scroll clean, as they had done to his?

How long could I survive as queen?

To win at cards takes more than one queen. So I strengthened my hand by drawing from my decks. I won the loyalty of the squadron leaders by offering them seats at my council table. Together, we held all the cards.

Fortune smiled upon us, and we won pot after pot. Before long, we owned every wave of South China's seas — and all who chanced upon them.

But Earth is more than wind and wave, is it not? I spun Fortune's wheel again, and this time she steered my ships toward land. Before we'd even stepped ashore, wealthy seaside towns turned their pockets inside out.

With their coin, I conquered poorer towns. I hired their masons and their carpenters. Their farmers and their fishermen. Seamstresses, scholars, spies — they all filled their rice bowls from my tubs.

On land and sea, we rivaled the emperor himself.
He sent an armada to destroy us.

My Red Flag Fleet took sixty-three of the emperor's best ships.

His admiral, in shame, took his own life.

The next admiral tried to starve us out. But the peasants in the countryside were in our pocket. They stole across the bay in rowboats laden with sacks of rice. Our bowls — and bellies — stayed full.

The emperor paid British ships, and Dutch ships, and even ships from Portugal, to attack us.

It was to no avail. Fortune sailed with me.

Yet even pirate queens grow tired. Remember, I had never dreamed of the sea.

And there was a price on my head.

In the distance, scudding clouds spilled across the face of the Jade Rabbit, erasing it from the sky. I looked to my heart and saw the inkstone there grinding my bones back to soot and glue.

It was time.

I sailed into Canton's port on a gunboat. I stepped onshore,
leaving my weapons and crew behind, though I brought their
wives and children with me. I approached the governor-general's
palace in the same way I had left the city, in a company of women.

In exchange for my freedom and the freedom of my crew, I
offered to surrender the bulk of my ships.

The governor-general demanded them all.

My heart roared like a dragon in my chest.
I refused.
I returned to my ships, resigned to die as I
had lived — a pirate queen.

But Fortune had a different notion. She shook my bones in her lacquered cup and threw them against my cabin door — *rap, rap, rap.*

The governor-general had reconsidered his hand. And found it wanting.

I left Canton that day a free woman,
and a rich one.

In the end, I had written my own scroll,
using brine and blood as my ink.
I had never dreamed of the sea, but the sea,
it seemed, had dreamed of me.

AUTHOR'S NOTE

Scholars know relatively little about the Pirate Queen. There are almost no primary documents about her life.

To tell her story, therefore, I had to fill in the gaps. Where there was no information about her specifically, I used facts about the period in which she lived to close the circle.

The historical record, however, is clear on several key points. First, that the Pirate Queen was a real person, and that she was probably the most powerful pirate in history. At the height of her career, she essentially controlled the economy of the South China Sea. Even so, her given name has been lost to history. Zheng Yi Sao, as she is frequently called, means simply "Wife of Zheng Yi."

She was born in or around 1775, probably near the city of Canton (now Guangzhou). How she met Zheng Yi is uncertain, as is the exact date of their marriage, although it's often given as 1801.

Was she kidnapped by her future husband? There is no proof that she was, nor that she wasn't. What we do know is that it was common practice in that time and place for pirates to take women captive, and to occasionally marry their favorites. I used this fact — and the fact that Zheng Yi Sao later instituted strict rules on how pirates under her command had to treat female

captives — to construct the scenes in the first part of this book.

In 1802, Zheng Yi was just one of many pirates vying for supremacy in the South China Sea. He and Zheng Yi Sao brought other pirates into a confederation and organized them into six color-coded squadrons. Their fleet eventually achieved domination over the area.

Zheng Yi died in 1807, possibly in a typhoon, possibly during an unsuccessful battle. Zheng Yi Sao moved quickly to assert her own power. A skillful diplomat, she won support from each fleet's captain. She kept the largest fleet, the Red Flag Fleet, for herself, placing its day-to-day operations under the command of Zhang Bao.

Zheng Yi Sao maintained power over her pirates by enforcing a strict code of conduct. Disobeying a superior or stealing from the pirates' own coffers meant immediate beheading. Female captives had to be treated respectfully; if pirates chose to marry, they had to remain faithful to their wives. Zheng Yi Sao also initiated rigorous new business practices, including an elaborate system for sharing booty (stolen riches).

With much of South China's coast now under her control, Zheng Yi Sao became the de facto government of the region. She set up tax offices, issued permits to would-be traders and collected fees from ship captains to ensure safe passage. She backed up her rule with military might and strategic cleverness. Her measures were so effective that sometimes sailors in the Cantonese army even sabotaged their own ships rather than go against her in battle.

Zheng Yi Sao seemed invulnerable. But a threat simmered within her own ranks: infighting among the fleets' commanders. With great foresight, she decided to "abandon ship." On April 8, 1810, she entered into a tense series of negotiations with Pai Ling, the governor-general of Liang-kuang.

On April 20, 1810, the deal was done. Zheng Yi Sao had arranged for the successful surrender of 17,318 pirates, 226 boats and 1,315 cannon — and her own freedom. She also managed to secure 120 junks (Chinese sailing ships) for Zhang Bao — both for his personal use and for deployment in the lucrative salt trade. She retired from her life at sea, married Zhang Bao, had one son and lived to the ripe age of sixty-nine.

Until recently, Zheng Yi Sao's astonishing career was known to only a few historians. This story, I hope, will introduce this amazing woman to a wider audience.

SOURCES

Murray, Dian. "One Woman's Rise to Power: Cheng I's Wife and the Pirates." *Historical Reflections/Reflexions Historiques*, Vol 8, No. 3, Women in China: Current Directions in Historical Scholarship (Fall 1981) pp. 147–161.

Murray, Dian. *Pirates of the South China Coast, 1790-1810*. Stanford University Press, 1987.

Szczepanski, Kallie. "Zheng Shi, Pirate Lady of China." ThoughtCo, Jan. 23, 2018, thoughtco.com/zheng-shi-pirate-lady-of-china-195617.

FURTHER REFERENCES

Ching Shih Information https://chingshih-info.weebly.com/

The Fearless Life of Ching Shih #OrdinaryWomen. https://www.youtube.com/watch?v=t0U6Ol-38Tw

"The Most Successful Pirate of All Time — Dian Murray." TedEd. https://ed.ted.com/lessons/the-most-successful-pirate-of-all-time-dian-murray

Yolen, Jane. *Sea Queens: Women Pirates around the World*. Illustrated by Christine Joy Pratt. Charlesbridge, 2008.

A NOTE ON THE NAMES IN THIS BOOK

It was difficult to choose the spelling for the names of the people in this book. There are several systems for writing Chinese words in Roman characters. In this book, I opted to use the pinyin names *Zheng Yi Sao*, *Zheng Yi* and *Zhang Bao*. You can also find the pirate queen's name spelled as Ching Shih and Cheng I Sao. Zheng Yi's name is sometimes spelled as Cheng I, while Zhang Bao's name is sometimes written as Cheung Po Tsai or Chang Pao.